Nor

Summer Holiday

JAMES SUTHERLAND

Chapter 1

It was the middle of July and the sun shone brightly down on Finbar's field. Bumble bees were busy bumbling, gathering sweet-smelling pollen from the clover which was in full bloom. In the hedgerows, sparrows chattered and blackbirds chirruped; in the undergrowth beetles beetled about as only beetles know how.

"Colin?" Norbert, the fat old horse, was standing in his favourite spot beneath the old sycamore tree, peering up into the branches in search of his feathery pal, Colin the cuckoo.

"Yes?" came an irritable voice from above.

"Are you there?"

"Well Norbert - either *I* am here, or *you* are hearing things – I'll leave it up to you to decide."

Confused, Norbert stood in silence for a moment, frowning as he pondered his friend's words. *Was Colin there or not?* Unsure what to do next, he about to trot back across the field to the spot where he had been grazing, when a familiar voice again filtered down through the greenery.

"And to what do I owe the pleasure of your company on this fine morning?"

Norbert smiled one of his biggest horsey smiles. *Colin WAS there after all!*

"Well," he whinnied happily "I was feeling a bit bored, so I thought I'd come and see what you were up to."

"Impossible."

Now Norbert was *even more* confused.

"I'm sorry Colin," he frowned "but I don't understand."

There followed a violent rustling of branches and the cuckoo's beaky face appeared among the branches just above his head.

"I was merely pointing out that it is quite impossible for a creature of your intellect to be bored."

"Oh? Why's that?"

"For the simple reason that, in order for someone to be bored, they must first be in possession of a *brain*. And it is here, my dearest friend, that you are found wanting."

More baffled than ever, Norbert returned to his original question.

"So what *are* you up to, Colin?" he said simply.

"If you must know, I *was* reading."

"Oh," Norbert beamed. This came as no surprise - Colin was *always* reading. *Perhaps that was why he was so clever.* "What are you reading?" he persisted.

"Before I was rudely interrupted, I *was* reading what is commonly referred to as a *travel brochure.*"

"Oh."

Colin shot him one of his fiercest glares.

"Will you *please* refrain from repeating the word 'Oh' every ten seconds?" he clucked. "It is possibly *the* most annoying of your *many, many* annoying habits!"

"I'm sorry Colin," Norbert replied. "What's a *travel badger* anyway?"

"Not *badger,* you cloth-eared nincompoop! A *brochure.* It's a kind of magazine that helps people decide where they might like to go on holiday."

"Oh."

"Grrrrrr!"

"Are *you* going to go on a holiday, Colin?" Norbert smiled, happily oblivious to his friend's growing irritation.

"I am considering it, yes. As you yourself have just said, life in this particular field does tend to get rather boring, and I feel the need for a change of scene."

At this, Norbert's smile faded; *if Colin went away, even for a short while, life in the field just wouldn't be the same…*

"Where are you thinking of going?" he frowned.

"I haven't decided just yet. It says in my *brochure* that the French Riviera is rather agreeable at this time of year - speaking of which, I must get back to my reading. Goodbye Norbert." And with these words, Colin's beaky visage vanished back into the dense foliage of the sycamore tree.

"Colin?" Norbert had always been very slow to take a hint.

"You rang?"

"Is it far to the French Riviera?"

"Did you ever study geography, Norbert?"

"No, Colin," the horse answered truthfully. *He hadn't the faintest idea what 'geography' was.*

"Well if you had, you would know that the French Riviera lies several hundred miles due south of here as the crow, or rather, the cuckoo, flies."

"Wow – that sounds like an awful long way away." Norbert now sounded *very* worried indeed. The last time he had seen Colin take to the air, it had only been on a short-haul journey to Finbar's farmhouse, which was less than a mile away, and even this had tested his feathered friend to his limits.

"And what do you mean by that?" Colin snapped, his angry face poking out once more from among the leaves.

Finally sensing that his friend was getting annoyed, Norbert tried his best to be diplomatic.

"Oh nothing, Colin," he gulped. "I'm sure you would be fine..."

"For once in your life, Norbert, you are correct!"

"But, I couldn't help thinking about that time you flew up to the farmhouse to get me a toothbrush…"

"Oh, you were, were you?" the cuckoo clucked. "And what of it?"

"Well, it's just that the farmhouse is only over there and you did seem a little bit..." Norbert shuffled awkwardly on his hooves as he searched for a tactful word. "You seemed a little bit *tired,*" he said, finally.

This had Colin hopping up and down on his branch in fury."

"How *dare* you!" he squawked. "To think that you would have the *cheek* to suggest that I, Colin the cuckoo, would be incapable of making a simple journey to the French Riviera..."

"But..."

"Surely you have not forgotten that we cuckoos fly south for the winter?"

"No, but..."

"Enough, Norbert. Talking to you has helped to make up my mind. Tomorrow, I fly for the Riviera. Goodbye, my friend – and I *mean* it this time!"

Sadly, Norbert turned and began to plod back towards the corner of the field where the juiciest grass could be found. He had not travelled more than a few paces, however, when something very unusual happened: he had an idea. With a slight sense of trepidation, he turned and waddled back in the direction of the sycamore tree.

"Colin?" he cringed.

There was a muffled cry and a sharp rustling of branches before a ferocious face appeared from among the branches.

"What is it *now*?"

"Can *I* come on holiday with you?"

The cuckoo gave a violent start that almost sent him tumbling from his perch.

"*You?*" he gurgled, his face a mask of sheer horror. "Come on holiday with *me*? *Certainly not!*"

"But…"

"You've had some ridiculous ideas over the years, Norbert, but this just about takes the biscuit! *Whoever heard of a horse going on holiday, anyway?*"

"Ok Colin," Norbert agreed with a sigh.

"And whatever you do, *don't* go telling anyone about this – I want to slip away quietly without any fuss…"

Chapter 2

Farmer Finbar studied his reflection anxiously in the bathroom mirror. He was not what anyone would describe as a *vain* man who worried overly about his appearance – *what, after all was the point in washing one's face or brushing one's hair when the next item on the agenda was cleaning out the pigsty?* But today was different; today, he was expecting a very special visitor.

For almost a year, Finbar had nursed a secret love for a certain Mrs Muckleton. A widow who owned another farm across the valley, she was, in his opinion, the most beautiful woman ever to have walked the Earth. Whilst others may have pointed out that her hair was going a little grey, that her nose was an inch too long, or her bottom several sizes too big, to Finbar, these things were mere details which failed to dent her appeal. And today, Mrs Muckleton was due to pop round for the first time ever in order to return a chainsaw that she had borrowed the previous week.

All his life, Finbar had been too busy with his farm to devote much time or thought to the subject of women. To him, they had always seemed something of a mysterious, even alien, species; those that he met in the village appeared to be mostly interested in chattering among themselves and spending lots of money on strange and exotic objects such as clothes and shoes. Why – he had even once seen a woman buying something called *shampoo!* Finbar certainly didn't like the idea of anybody spending lots of *his* money, and so had always been careful to keep his distance. Until now. His love for

Mrs Muckleton had begun as a tiny seed that was planted in his heart the previous summer when he had witnessed her all-conquering performance in a pie-eating competition at the village fete. And from this seed, his love had blossomed to such a degree that he was now ready to give her his heart. *He would,* he had decided, *make Mrs Muckleton his wife if it was the last thing he did!*

Ever since that day at the village fete, however, he had been content to allow their relationship to develop at its own pace; he had lived on his own for thirty-nine years – another few months surely wouldn't matter. But suddenly the situation had taken a sinister turn; rumour had it that Mrs Muckleton had been spotted heading up the lane that led to Old Joe Baxter's farm. Finbar and Old Joe Baxter had long been bitter enemies, ever since a dispute some twenty years beforehand over the ownership of a small section of hedge which denoted the border between their respective farms.

Finbar considered Old Joe Baxter to be stupid, ugly and smelly. Old Joe, in turn, considered Finbar to be stupid, ugly and smelly. Their mutual dislike was such that, although they were neighbours, they never said so much as a word to one another if they could avoid it. And yet now, Finbar pondered bitterly as he ran a dirty old comb through the remaining few greasy strands of hair on his scalp, this man, this *fiend* in human form, was about to steal his one true love from right under his nose! As he applied copious amounts of talcum powder to his sweating armpits, Finbar knew that he must act now, or risk losing Mrs Muckleton to his deadly rival forever...

"Garn!" he exclaimed, glancing at his watch. It was almost five o'clock in the afternoon; *his beloved would be here at any moment!* With a final tweak of his stubby little moustache, he tore himself away from the mirror and hurried downstairs to check his sausages. Finbar was *extremely* fond of sausages, and he had, that very morning, purchased half-a-pound of Barry the Butcher's finest specimens with the intention of cooking them for Mrs Muckleton's breakfast. Sausages, he knew, were the way to *his* heart, so why should the same law of nature not apply with regard to members of the opposite sex? Flinging open the refrigerator door, he saw to his relief that they were still present and correct, looking as plump and bewitching as ever.

"There you are, my beauties," he slobbered, gazing at them adoringly.

"DING DONG," chimed the doorbell. *Mrs Muckleton had arrived.*

*

Alone in his field once again, Norbert trotted absent-mindedly over to the water trough for a drink. But just as he was about to take his first slurp, he was alerted to the sound of a motor vehicle coming down the lane. Raising his head to peer over the hedgerows, he was thrilled to see the outline of a Land rover rounding the bend – a Land rover towing the unmistakeable form of a small, pink horsebox.

"Delilah!" he whinnied joyfully. Delilah, for those of you are not up-to-date with Norbert's love-life, was the pretty pony who often came to graze in the next field. Norbert had, for a long time, been head-over-hooves in love with her, though she had never, to date, shown any signs of wanting to return his affection.

Transfixed, he watched as a man hopped down from the car and unfastened the ramp, his eyes widening in awe as Delilah emerged, looking more gorgeous and graceful than ever, her dappled fur gleaming in the summer sunshine.

It was but a matter of moments before the man, having fastened up the horsebox, clambered back into the car and revved the engine. Seconds later, he had disappeared off around the bend in the lane and the two horses were alone.

"Yoo hoo!" Delilah called cheerfully. "Norbert – is that you?" Whenever she had been away to a horse show, she was always anxious to catch up on all the latest gossip from Finbar's field.

"Hi Delilah," Norbert beamed. "Yes, it's me. I'm glad you've come back because Colin's going away tomorrow…" *He stopped mid-sentence. Had Colin said something about wanting to slip away without any fuss? He couldn't quite remember…*

He was too late – once Delilah had the slightest nugget of gossip, there was no way she would let it rest until she had the full story.

"Going away?" she smiled. intrigued. "What do you mean, going away?"

"Well," Norbert cringed "he's going on holiday, but he told me not to tell anybody."

"Not tell anyone?" Delilah snorted. "Why ever not?"

"I erm… I don't know."

"Come on, Norbert – the sight of that fat old buzzard taking to the skies is something no one in their right mind would want to miss. I'll see you later."

"But where are you going?" Norbert gulped.

"Why – I'm off to spread the word, of course – this is guaranteed to be prime box-office entertainment!"

*

"Mrs Muckleton!" Finbar grovelled as he ushered his visitor into the hallway. "I must say it's *luverly* to see you, *most* luverly..."

"Hello Mr Finbar," she replied in her deep and husky voice*. "I've come to return your chainsaw." * *Author's note: do not, reader, be fooled into thinking that Mrs Muckleton's voice was deep and husky in a sensual sort of way; it was deep and husky in the same way that an ogre or perhaps a troll's voice would be deep and husky – sinister and unpleasant, if you see what I'm getting at...*

"You shouldn't have, Mrs Muckleton, really you shouldn't," the farmer cooed like a turtle dove.

"Oh but I *did*. You see, Mr Finbar, I'm afraid it's broken."

"*Broken?*" Finbar cried. "How do you mean, broken?" *He had loved that chainsaw like a brother...*

"Well, there's no need to get so upset, Mr Finbar," she snapped right back at him. "Goodness me – it's only a rusty old piece of junk."

"Rusty old piece of junk?" the farmer bristled, his face reddening.

"Absolutely. To be honest, I am most disappointed that you had the gall to lend me something that was clearly faulty."

"Faulty? But..."

"Faulty indeed – do you know, the blade snapped almost as soon as I started cutting up my old tractor..."

"*Tractor!*" Finbar gasped, his chubby cheeks now a deep shade of purple. "But Mrs Muckleton, that there chainsaw was meant for chopping *logs!*"

"Nonsense – it was clearly faulty. I hope you realize I could have been seriously injured when that blade snapped..."

"But..."

"And I shall look forward to receiving an apology from you in due course."

With steam now coming out of his ears, his face black with fury, Finbar took a deep breath and counted to ten before replying.

"Of course, Mrs Muckleton," he grimaced, finally. "I'm ever so sorry about that. How silly of me to get all worked up over a silly ole chainsaw…"

Mrs Muckleton looked him up and down, her expression a mixture of triumph and distain.

"Very well," she growled. "Apology accepted. I've left the chainsaw in your front yard for you to dispose of as you see fit. Now, if you don't mind, I must bid you farewell." And with these words, she turned and marched back out through the front door, her enormous bottom jiggling like an oversized sack of potatoes as she went.

"But Mrs Muckleton!" Finbar wailed after her. "I've got some beautiful sausages in the fridge. I was going to cook 'em for our breakfast!"

The woman stopped in her tracks. *Finbar held his breath. Would the sausages work their magic?*

"I'm *terribly* sorry," she replied with a smirk "but I'm having breakfast up at Old Joe Baxter's this evening. He's having a barbeque."

"A *barbeque*?" Finbar had never been to a barbeque; they remained a thing of exotic mystery as far as he was concerned.

"Yes. He's had the yard at his farm converted into a beautiful patio with its own brick barbeque. We're having fillet steaks, venison burgers, chicken kebabs... "

"Fillet steaks? Venison burgers? Chicken kebabs?" Finbar reeled, clutching at the doorframe for support. *Just when Mrs Muckleton had almost been in his grasp, that wily rascal Old Joe Baxter had out-foxed him again!*

"Goodbye Mr Finbar. No doubt I shall see you around the village in the near future."

The farmer did not reply; it was all he could do to goggle in helpless despair as he watched his one true love disappearing off down the lane in the direction of Old Joe Baxter's farm.

"Garn!" he muttered to nobody in particular as her plump posterior vanished around the bend.

Chapter 3

When the sun appeared above the horizon the next morning, it was greeted with a loud *PLOP!*

'What on Earth are you talking about?' you cry.

Well, reader, the loud *PLOP* to which I refer is the sound that an overweight cuckoo makes when descending from a sycamore tree. Unlike many other birds which can take off from a position high up in the branches, Colin's lack of match-fitness meant that he could only hope to get airborne by taking a long run-up across the ground, a bit like a jumbo jet.

As she had promised, Delilah had spread the word of his planned departure and, as expected, a whole host of animals had gathered in the field, all chattering excitedly and jostling among themselves for the best front-row seats. On the five-bar gate, nine sparrows were huddled together with a trio of blackbirds and a plump woodpigeon. Other eager spectators among the hundreds present included a weasel named Steve, Roger the frog, a chicken called Dave, plus a field mouse who went by the name of Miguel. Even the Badger family, who usually retired to their set, deep below the roots of the hedge at dawn, had made a special effort to stay awake in order to witness the main event. Norbert, of course, was also present, though he did not share the others' excitement; he didn't like the idea of his dearest friend flying off to a distant land, whence he might never return.

Colin, for his part, was furious with Norbert. He had clearly stated his desire to slip away quietly, with a minimum of fuss; though he would never openly admit it, he was himself a little worried about his aeronautical abilities, and would have much preferred to conduct his take-off in private rather than in front of a huge, baying crowd. Now, thanks to Norbert's big mouth, every creature within a ten-mile radius was here to witness it!

"For goodness' sake!" he cried, noticing a small but enterprising hedgehog setting up an ice cream stand in one corner of the field.

"Norbert! This is *all your* fault! I shan't be sending you a postcard after this!"

"That's ok, Colin," Norbert replied glumly. "I can't read anyway."

"Well," the bird retorted with growing agitation "as long as you understand that even if you *could* read, I still wouldn't send you a postcard!"

"Yes, Colin. I understand."

"Anyway – Enough of this idle chit-chat. Clear the runway whilst I prepare for take-off."

"Colin?"

"What is it *now*, Norbert?"

"What's a runway?"

"It's a long strip of tarmac used by aircraft for taking off and landing."

"Oh." Norbert rotated his enormous, long head from side to side. As far as he could see, there wasn't anything in his field that could be described as a long strip of tarmac; there was just a lot of grass.

"There *is* no actual runway, you nitwit!" Colin snapped. "I was speaking *figuratively*. I meant that I wanted you to move some of those pesky animals out of the way so I have room to take a good run-up."

Obediently, Norbert waddled to and fro through the crowd until a sufficiently long stretch of grass had been cleared. Meanwhile, Colin began to limber up, stretching his wings and wiggling his bottom as he flexed his long, crooked tail feathers, doing his best to ignore the rising sniggers from the watching throng. *Fools* he thought, bitterly. *I shall have the last laugh when I'm sunning myself on the French Riviera.*

"Farewell, my friends!" he cried, defiantly. "Or perhaps I should say *au revoir*, as they say in France..."

And with these fateful words, he began to taxi along the narrow strip of grass. The crowd drew their breath in anticipation as, with a flurry of feathers, the corpulent cuckoo slowly but surely began to gather speed…

Chapter 4

It has been the subject of much debate among those who witnessed Colin's take-off whether, had Farmer Finbar bothered to trim the enormous hedge that surrounded his field, the luckless cuckoo might have gained sufficient height to clear its upper branches.

Unfortunately, Norbert's field was screened from the farmhouse by a small patch of woodland, known as a *copse*, which meant that forgetful old Finbar would sometimes go for weeks on end without giving the hedge-cutting so much as a second thought. As a result of his neglect, the hedge over which Colin was attempting to fly that morning had been left to develop into a kind of natural Berlin Wall of twisted, dense and spiky foliage. Though he had flapped and fluttered his aged wings for all they were worth, the beleaguered bird had never stood a chance...

As luck would have it, there had been a squirrel on hand who was trained in first aid and was able to treat him at the scene. Alas, in spite of Lesley's best efforts (for that was the squirrel's name), Colin, though alive, was badly shaken and his plumage a mess, with many feathers lost to the brambles in the hedge, and the few that remained, sticking out at right angles from his battered body. Try, reader, to picture a chicken that has been half-plucked and then pummelled with a cricket bat, and you will get a good idea of how Colin looked after his crash.

Worst of all, however, was the very public humiliation he had suffered. Though he had never had many friends, Colin had always liked to imagine himself as a highly respected member of the community, yet he feared that the day's events had changed all of that in an instant. From now on, he would no longer be seen as 'Colin the Wise,' but rather 'Colin the Clown," the hapless fool who could not even fly over a simple hedge without making a spectacle of himself. *And it was all because of Norbert and that big mouth of his...*

And so, his body aching, his pride in tatters, Colin had concluded that there was only one course of action open to him; he would return to the sanctuary of his nest, and there he would remain in splendid solitude, shut off from the cruel world and all of its troubles, until such time as his wounds, both physical and psychological, had healed.

*

"Colin?" As soon as the crowds had dispersed, Norbert waddled over to the old sycamore tree, anxious to check on the welfare of his friend.

"Go away - I'm not here."

"Oh." Norbert considered this for a moment. "Are you *sure* you're not there?" he ventured uncertainly.

"Yes, Norbert – I've never been more certain of anything in my life. Now if you don't mind, you can shove off and pester somebody else for a change."

"Ok, Colin."

And so, with a heavy heart, the old horse turned and walked away. He thought about going to look for Delilah, but then remembered that what had happened to his friend was partly her fault, so he wandered instead down to the badgers' hole underneath the hedge. Jason, the youngest in the litter, was usually game for a bit of fun.

"Jason?" he called, pressing his snout as far as it would go into the dark opening. No response. "*JASON*?" he repeated louder. Still no response. Norbert was about to call a third time when he heard a sharp, scuffling sound somewhere in the depths of the hole. Seconds later a ferocious black-and-white stripy face appeared.

"What the *dickens* do you think you are doing?" It was Jason's dad, Mr Badger, and he seemed extremely upset about something.

"I was just wondering if Jason wanted to come out to play."

"Out to play? Are you stark-raving mad?"

"No," Norbert replied, somewhat taken aback. "At least, I don't think so…"

"Have you forgotten that we badgers are *nocturnal* creatures?"

"No – I knew that. Colin told me just the other day."

"Then why are here, bellowing into our hole, when the sun is high in the sky?"

"Well," Norbert said simply "I *did* know that you were nocturnal, but I'm afraid I'd forgotten what it meant."

At this, Mr Badger let out what can only be described as a blood-curdling snarl before vanishing back down his hole.

Very often, when somebody is overcome with despair, they will look to the heavens, and this is precisely what Norbert now proceeded to do. For a moment, he was dazzled by the sun, but as he blinked his long eyelashes, something caught his eye. Way, way up high, so high that it was little more than a white speck against the deep blue summer sky, he saw a bird, circling over the field. As his eyes focused, Norbert could see that it was a very large bird, with wings that were at least twice the span of Colin's.

Strange he pondered. He knew most, if not all of the birds who lived in the vicinity, and he was certain that this was not one of them.

"Maybe if I call out to him, he'll come down and talk to me for a bit," he thought to himself. And so, with his huge neck raised to the heavens, Norbert whinnied his loudest whinny. To his delight, after a brief moment of hesitation, he saw the circling bird beginning its slow and graceful descent…

Chapter 5

Farmer Finbar scratched his stubbly chin as he surveyed the yard outside his farmhouse. As his beady eyes scanned from left to right, they noted the following exhibits:

Two worn-out tractor tyres.
One rusty bike – wheels missing.
Three large clumps of nettles.
One broken refrigerator.
One Wellington boot with a hole in the toe.
One soiled mattress.
One medium-sized heap of rotten horse manure.

"Garn!" he exclaimed. It had suddenly dawned on Finbar that perhaps *his* yard did not compare favourably to that which belonged to Old Joe Baxter as a romantic location in which to woo a lady of Mrs Muckleton's refinement; indeed, it put him at a grave disadvantage. *If he were to stand any chance of winning the heart of his beloved, he would need to raise his game considerably.*

Thus, it was with an air of grim determination that he clambered aboard his tractor and chugged off down the lane to Lower Bottomton, the nearest village. *Old Joe Baxter wasn't the only one around here who could build patios with brick barbeques...*

An hour later, he was back, his trailer laden with fifty concrete paving slabs, three bags of cement, and half-a-tonne of builder's sand. Usually, in his day-to-day chores around the farm, Finbar was careful to fit in as many tea breaks as possible. Today, however, things were different; the thought that Mrs Muckleton might, even now, be sitting on Old Joe Baxter's patio, gorging herself on fillet steaks and venison burgers, was almost enough to send him insane with jealousy.

Unloading the trailer was a gruelling task; the concrete slabs were extremely heavy, and the builder's sand had an uncanny knack of finding its way into his mouth and hair. But, like a man possessed, Finbar continued in his toil, heedless of any discomfort, barely pausing for breath until all fifty of the slabs, together with the three bags of cement and the mountain of sand, were piled neatly at one end of the yard. There is much truth in the saying, reader, that jealousy can be a powerful motivator of men....

His plan was to spread the sand evenly across the floor of his yard with a shovel, before laying the slabs on top. Once this was done, he would add the cement to hold the slabs firmly in place. *Yes... Tomorrow evening, HE would be the one inviting Mrs Muckleton to a barbeque, and Old Joe Baxter would be laughing on the other side of his face...*

It was as he trudged across the yard to fetch his shovel that Finbar heard the sound. It was a sound not unlike the sort you would normally expect to hear around an African watering hole at dawn; yes, reader – Finbar's big, fat, empty stomach was grumbling!

"Garn!" he grunted. "It's nearly bedtime and I haven't even had me tea! I'd better eat up them there sausages before they go past their sell-by date. I can always get some more from Barry the Butcher for me barbeque tomorrow."

With this, he downed tools for the night and trudged wearily into the farmhouse to turn on the grill.

*

So exhausted was Farmer Finbar that night, that he slept like someone who has been hit with a brick, not moving so much as a finger until the cockerel crowed at daybreak. As the mists of sleep cleared, the events of the previous day came back to him in a flash.

"I must get to work on that there patio!" he cried, springing like a gazelle from beneath the eiderdown. A fat, out-of-condition gazelle, but a gazelle nonetheless. Hurriedly pulling on his trousers, he blundered across to the window and threw open the curtains in order to inspect his yard.

Ah yes – the concrete slabs were where he had left them, stacked neatly and ready to be laid out across the yard. So too were the bags of cement. But of the builder's sand, there was no trace.

Finbar blinked. *Was he still in his bed having a bad dream? This couldn't be true...*

He pinched himself. *Ouch!*

He pinched himself harder. *Double ouch!* There was simply no denying that he was wide awake, and that somebody had stolen his precious sand during the night. And as to the identity of that somebody, Finbar had a very good idea...

"Garn!" he roared. *"It'll be that Old Joe Baxter! Just wait 'til I get my 'ands on 'im!"*

*

"My dearest Finbar," Baxter grinned through his yellow, crooked teeth. "You are forgetting yourself! A sophisticated gentleman like me, stealing sand in the

middle of the night from the likes of *you?*
You must be out of your tiny mind!"

"*Tiny mind?* Why, you..."

"Why on *earth* would I need building
sand anyway? Haven't you heard? *My* patio
is already up and running and is the talk of
the village." Old Joe Baxter drew himself up
to his full height, towering over his much-
shorter rival. Finbar's physique, reader, was
similar to that of the little teapot in the
famous nursery rhyme: short and stout.

"You pinched it 'cos you reckoned I was
going to have a better patio than yours!"
Finbar bellowed, defiantly.

"Nonsense! You make the mistake of
assuming that we are all as petty-minded as

yourself, Finbar. Now, if you don't mind popping along - I need to go into the village to pay a visit to Barry the butcher. You see, Mrs Muckleton has agreed to join me tonight for *another* barbeque and I'm clean out of venison steaks..."

"*Garn!*"

Chapter 6

Meanwhile, tucked away behind the wooded copse, Norbert glanced around his field with decidedly mixed feelings. The seagull (for it was such a bird that he had spotted high in the sky the previous evening) had proven to be blessed with an extremely kind nature. Having alighted on the grass between Norbert's enormous hooves, it had listened very patiently as the horse had related the sorry tale of Colin's ill-fated attempt to fly to the French Riviera, right through to the current predicament with his refusal to come down from his nest. The tale thus concluded, the great bird had spent several minutes, strutting back and forth through the grass as he considered the best plan of action. When he was finally ready to address the unhappy horse, the conversation had proceeded as follows:

"Mmmm," the seagull sighed with a sympathetic shake of the head. "It seems to me as though there has been a serious breakdown in diplomatic relations between yourself and the cuckoo. Luckily for you, I am here..."

"Oh?"

"Allow me to introduce myself; my name is Captain Charles Clarington-Smith and I am a member of a secret organisation. Have you ever heard of the *SAS*?"

"No."

"It stands for 'Seagull and Seagull.' It is an organisation *so* exclusive that there is only myself and my brother, Clive, in it."

Norbert merely stared at him blankly, unable to see how any of this would help him tempt Colin down from his tree.

Captain Smith fixed him with a crafty grin. "Listen carefully," he squawked "for I have already formulated a *brilliant* plan that is guaranteed to succeed."

"Really?" Norbert's was astonished – he had *never, ever* in his entire life come up with a plan, brilliant or otherwise.

"Yes – it's perfectly simple," the seagull continued. "If your feathered friend is unable to reach the French Riviera, then the only alternative is for *us* to bring the French Riviera to *him*!"

"But how can we do that if we don't even know what it looks like?"

"Ha!" the Captain chuckled. "*You* may not know what it looks like – *I*, on the other hand, know it like the back of my wing, having been there many times. Allow me to paint you a picture of that beautiful place…"

Norbert listened in wonderment as the Captain proceeded to describe the South of France in such detail, that by the time he had finished, he almost felt as though he had been there himself.

"It sounds nice," he said as the bird fell silent "but how can we bring it *here*?"

"Fear, not my dear fellow," the Captain smiled. "Do you remember when you called me down here?"

"Yes."

"Well – the reason I was circling so high up in the sky was that I was carrying out some detailed reconnaissance of the area."

"Oh?"

"Absolutely – and while I was up there, I spotted a few things that will be of great use to us in the task ahead. Indeed, I can state with confidence that *all* of the vital materials we need to transform this field into an *exact* replica of the French Riviera can be obtained within a mere few hundred metres of this very spot..."

*

In order to turn a field into a beach it is, of course, essential to have at your disposal a large quantity of sand. By a stroke of good fortune, a large quantity of sand was one of the many things that Captain Charles Clarington-Smith had spotted whilst circling high above Finbar's Farm. For a creature with his military background, it had been the simplest of tasks to commandeer an army of ants and set them to work. All through the night the tiny creatures had toiled whilst the farmer was fast asleep in his bed, removing his precious sand, grain by grain from the yard, transporting it down through the wooded copse to its final destination at the bottom of Norbert's field.

At daybreak, the seagull once again took to the skies to obtain an aerial view of the work in progress. Although the ants could not be faulted for their monumental efforts, the Captain, when he landed back on the grass beside Norbert, was obliged to report that the 'beach' in its present form, was less than satisfactory.

The crux of the problem, he explained, was the sheer *size* of the terrain; because Norbert's field was so big, the pile of building sand which had looked so huge in Finbar's yard was sufficient to provide only the lightest dusting over the long grass. Somehow, by hook or by crook, they simply *had* to obtain more sand if the mission was to have any chance of success...

Chapter 7

Little did Norbert and Captain Clarington-Smith know that, at the very moment they were wondering where they could find more sand, Farmer Finbar was trundling down the lane towards the village in his tractor in order to purchase a further half-tonne of the stuff. Though he had not been able to pin any formal evidence on the blighter Baxter, his rival was still the chief suspect for the previous night's skulduggery, and Finbar was more determined than ever to see the construction of his patio through to the bitter end.

We can thus imagine his dismay when, on his arrival at the builder's yard, he was informed by the owner, a certain Mr Yates, that he was clean out of building sand.

"Garn!"

"I'm sorry, Finbar," Mr Yates shook his head sympathetically "but it seems like Old Joe Baxter has started something of a patio-building craze in these parts. Everybody in the village wants one, and I just can't keep up with the demand!"

"Garn!"

Burning with indignation, Finbar was about to hop back up onto his tractor when the proprietor spoke again.

"I do know where you might find some, though," he whispered in a conspiratorial tone.

"Oh?" Finbar halted, hope burgeoning in his heart.

"Yes," Mr Yates continued. "I've 'eard on the grapevine that there might be half-a-tonne still available over at Old Pete Mitchell's yard in Flickton."

"Flickton!" Finbar cried. "That's nearly twenty miles away! It'll take me all afternoon to get over there and back in me tractor!"

But even as he spoke, he knew he had no choice; *either he must complete his patio or he would surely lose Mrs Muckleton forever...*

*

By the time Finbar chugged back into his yard, it was late in the afternoon. Fortunately, the intelligence handed down to him by Mr Yates had been spot on; Old Pete Mitchell had indeed possessed half-a-tonne of building sand, though he had, to Finbar's considerable fury, insisted on charging him more than twice the usual price for it.

"It's all about supply and demand," Old Pete had explained apologetically. "You know, *market forces* and all that..."

"Garn!"

Red faced and soaking with sweat, Finbar immediately set to work unloading his trailer. Though he huffed and he puffed and he puffed and he huffed, by the time the sand was piled next to the concrete slabs and cement, dusk was already creeping in. Mopping his brow, the exhausted farmer groaned with anguish as he was forced to concede that he would not be able to complete the patio before darkness fell. *But what if that rascal Old Joe Baxter came along in the dead of night and pinched his sand again?* One solution would be to stay up all night and stand guard, but Finbar knew that if he were to do this, he would be too tired to begin work the following morning...

For several minutes, he stood wringing his grubby hands in despair before an idea struck him. *Even if he couldn't finish the patio, he could at least spread his sand out all around the yard before it got dark; this way, if that Old Joe Baxter wanted to steal it, he would have to creep about in the pitch blackness, scraping it up with a shovel, a noisy activity which would be guaranteed to arouse him from his slumber.* And so, with a fresh glint of determination in his piggy eyes, Finbar picked up his spade and set to work.

"Ah yes," he muttered to himself as he clambered into bed. "I'll get 'im sure enough if he tries any of 'is funny business tonight!"

*

And yet, reader, in spite of his confident prediction, it will not surprise you to learn that when Farmer Finbar thrust open his curtains the following morning, every last grain of sand had been removed from the yard. There is probably no need for me to tell you what it was that he roared through the open window on making this unfortunate discovery, but I will do so anyway...

"GAAAAAAAAAAARN!"

Chapter 8

The fact that Finbar's sand had been spread out all around his yard had, of course, not made even the teeniest, tiniest difference to Captain Charles Clarington-Smith's army of ants. Just as they had done the previous night, they had streamed up through the wooded copse in their thousands, working steadily away over a period of several hours until every single grain had been transferred down to Norbert's field.

"Now then, Norbert," the seagull beamed as he surveyed their handiwork. "I think you'll agree that the second batch of sand has worked wonders. Why, if I didn't know better, I could easily believe that I was sunning myself down on the Riviera right now!"

Norbert, though, looked decidedly dubious. It was true that his field was beginning to resemble a beach, yet even Norbert was sufficiently intelligent to realize that there was still something missing.

"But what about the *sea*?" he whinnied, his voice filled with worry. "Didn't you say something about there being a big puddle of water called 'the sea' on the French Riviera?"

"My *dear fellow*, you are right!" the seagull agreed. "You need not fear, however, as I have already taken the necessary steps to provide you with a sea which will put the one on the Riviera to shame!"

"Oh?"

"Yes – you see, I have a mole in Finbar's farmyard."

"A mole?"

"Yes – it's a word that humans sometimes use when they are referring to a *spy,* except *my* mole happens to be an *actual* mole." Noticing Norbert's growing confusion, he continued hurriedly. "Anyway, this mole has provided me with intelligence which indicates that there is, in Finbar's yard, a water tap and a coil of hosepipe. Acting upon this, I have already despatched your friend, Jason the badger, on a daring mission to get this hosepipe and run it down through the wooded copse and into this very field."

"Oh."

"As soon as it is in position, I intend to fly up to the yard myself and turn on the tap." Hearing a loud rustling noise nearby, the Captain gestured towards the edge of the copse with his beak.

"Look – here he is now. Hello, my good fellow!"

Norbert peered round in time to see Jason's stripy form emerging from the wood. Sure enough, in his sharp teeth, he clutched the end of a green rubber hose. Satisfied that everything was in place, the captain bid them farewell and, beating his enormous wings, flew off up to the farmhouse in order to turn on the tap.

When he arrived at the yard, all was quiet, Finbar having already sallied forth to confront Old Joe Baxter about his latest suspected felony. Like much of the machinery on the farm, the tap was old and rusty, and the seagull had a terrible time trying to loosen it using only his pink webbed feet and his beak. The Captain, however, was not one to give up easily, and after several minutes of heroic perseverance, the tap suddenly turned and spluttered into life, the seagull taking to the air with a squawk of satisfaction as the first gurgle of water began its long journey down to Norbert's field.

*

"Colin?"
No response.
"Colin?"
No response.
"Colin?"
No response.
"Are you there, Colin?"
Like most birds, cuckoos do not have teeth as such. And yet, from the vicinity of the cuckoo's nest, high up in the leafy sycamore tree, a definite *gnashing* sound filtered down to Norbert's ears.
"Perhaps if you would allow me," the Captain suggested, fluttering his way up onto Norbert's back. "I have specialised training in the art of negotiation."

"My name," he bellowed, cupping his wing into a shape which was vaguely reminiscent of a loud hailer "is Captain Clarington-Smith. I am your friend."

"No you're not!" clucked a familiar voice from above. "I've never met you before in my life!"

This guy's a tough cookie, the Captain thought to himself.

"I am here on behalf of your friend, Norbert," he continued, trying a different tactic.

"He's no friend of mine! Tell him to go and boil his head!"

Mmm the seagull mused. *This is going to be a bit trickier than I expected...*

"That's a pity..." he responded calmly.

"No it isn't!"

"Because Norbert has something *very special* to show you."

There followed what is sometimes referred to as a *pregnant* silence.

"You mean... Something like a *surprise*?"

"Yes - I think it is fair to say that he has a surprise for you."

There followed another lengthy silence whilst Colin weighed this up. It had been his intention to punish Norbert for as long as possible by remaining up in his nest and refusing to come down. But the negotiator had unwittingly found the one weakness in his armoury; Colin *loved* surprises...

"Tell me what it is first," he quacked, finally.

"I'm sorry, sir, but the only way you'll find out is if you come down from the tree."

With a great deal of rustling of leaves and snapping of twigs, Colin's plump form made its way hurriedly down through the branches of the old sycamore tree.

"Well?" he snapped as soon as he was safely on the ground. "What is it? It had better be g..." The cuckoo stopped dead mid-sentence, temporarily lost for words as he stared at the scenery around him. To his astonishment, a large portion of Finbar's field appeared to have been transformed into a sandy beach, and down in the south-west corner, a large expanse of water shimmered seductively in the July sunshine. Though not *quite* the French Riviera, it was as close as one could possibly hope for in the middle of the English countryside.

"Do you like it, Colin?" Norbert's voice betrayed his anxiety.

Colin *loved* it, though he was not going to give that clod-hopping old horse the satisfaction of knowing that this was the case just yet.

"It's ok, I suppose," he sniffed.

"Shall we go and walk on the sand, Colin?" A tiny hope of redemption flickered to life in Norbert's heart.

Colin was *desperate* to wiggle his toes in the sand, but again did his best to conceal his enthusiasm.

"Norbert," he sighed. "You have done me a terrible wrong by blabbing to Deilah..."

"I'm sorry, Colin."

The cuckoo looked at him, shaking his feathery head.

"I may live to regret it," he said with a sigh "but on this one occasion, I am prepared to let the matter drop."

"Do you mean," Norbert's eyes widened as he spoke "that you *forgive* me?"

"Yes, Norbert. I suppose I forgive you. I expect it's what Ghandi would have done, were he in my position. But *don't* go thinking that you can take advantage of my kind and gentle nature!"

"I won't, Colin, I promise..."

Chapter 9

It was a broken and deflated Farmer Finbar that clambered down from the seat of his tractor that afternoon. Once again, he had come off worst in what had been a bruising encounter with Old Joe Baxter. It *had*, however, more or less convinced him once and for all that Old Joe was *not* the person responsible for the crime.

Yet *someone* had stolen his precious sand, and it seemed more and more likely that this mysterious felon was going to get away with it! *How could he ever rest, knowing that the culprit was still at large and swanning about the place, free from justice?*

Exhausted in mind and body, Finbar was about to head up to his room for a lie down when he spotted something out of the ordinary in the corner of the yard; the old rusty tap had been connected up to a hose! *Stranger still, someone had turned the water on...*

"*Garn!*" he thundered. "If I follow this 'ere hosepipe, I'll *bet* it'll lead me straight to 'im wot's been nickin' me sand!" And so, his face as black as thunder, he stalked out of the yard, following the rubber hose as a Red Indian tracker would follow an enemy's footprints.

Fortunately for the multitude of animals in the field who had been enjoying the novelty of the beach, Finbar did not possess the lightness of foot of a Red Indian tracker, and the sound of his blundering approach through the wooded copse gave them ample time to remove themselves from the scene. All except for Norbert, of course; due to his enormous bulk, he had little choice but to stay put and await his master's arrival.

"Now I've got you!" Finbar roared as he charged out from among the trees, puffing and panting, his chubby cheeks bright red. But to his surprise, there was nobody there at all. Nobody, that is, apart for his old cart horse, Norbert.

Stranger still, his field appeared to have been transformed by an unseen hand into a beach of some kind... *But by whom?* Though he could never be described as an intelligent man, Finbar *was* at least intelligent enough to realize that there was no way on Earth that Norbert could be responsible...

As he stood, regaining his breath, scratching his head in bewilderment, the look of anger on Finbar's features slowly began to clear. *So what if he didn't have a patio... He had a BEACH! Old Joe Baxter didn't have a beach! Just wait until Mrs Muckleton saw this!*

And so off he went in search of his beloved. *Compared with a beach, the concept of a patio suddenly seemed very boring indeed...*

*

"Oh Norbert! Cooey!"

Recognizing the familiar voice, Norbert pricked up his ears. *Delilah!* Having a short memory, he had already forgotten about all the trouble she had caused, and so was delighted to see her again.

"Hello Delilah," he replied, trotting over to the five-bar gate.

"Gosh, Norbert! Look at your field - it's *beautiful!*" she whinnied with delight.

Norbert's heart pounded in his chest with pride.

"Have *you* done this?" she purred. "Why Norbert – I never knew you were so clever!"

Norbert's heart pounded even harder. *For as long as he lived, he would never forget today; the first time ever in his life that he had been described by anybody as 'clever'.*

"Can I come in?" she pleaded, fluttering her long eyelashes for all she was worth.

"I'd like you to, Delilah," Norbert replied, his face clouding with worry "but I don't know how to open this gate."

"You are so *silly* sometimes," Delilah giggled. "Have you forgotten that you are looking at the best show-jumping pony in the county? Stand back – I'm coming over!"

Norbert stood back as instructed and watched in awe as she cantered daintily in a circle around her paddock before charging at full speed towards the gate.

"See," she said, easily clearing the obstacle and alighting on the sand beside him.

"Wow!" Norbert gasped. "I didn't know you could do that. How come you've never been over to my side of the gate before now?"

"Because, my darling," she smiled "you've never had a beach before now. Come on - last one in the sea is a rotten egg!" And before Norbert could reply, she galloped down the field, crossed the sand, and plunged into the water.

*

In theory, Captain Charles Clarington-Smith's plan to partially flood Norbert's field had been a good one; nobody could argue that the lake, glistening as it did that day in the sunshine, didn't *look* very appealing to the eye. Where the plan came somewhat unstuck, however, was that it did not take into account what conditions would be like just *below* the shimmering surface. What the seagull had *not* known was that, when a field floods with water, it does *not* miraculously transform itself into an ideal bathing facility; it transforms itself into a foul quagmire of black, sticky mud. And it was in the midst of this foul quagmire of black, sticky mud that Delilah now found herself floundering...

"Norbert!" she sobbed when she had finally extricated herself. "Norbert, you *brute!* You tricked me into your field on purpose, knowing *full well* that I'd sink into that nasty, horrid mud! I shall *never, ever* speak to you again as long as I live!"

*

"Now then, Mrs Muckleton," Finbar smirked as he led the woman of his dreams down through the little wooded copse later that afternoon. "I've got something *very special* to show you, but you *must* close your eyes until I say."

"*Really*, Mr Finbar," she snapped. "This is *most irregular*. I can't see for the life of me why you think you can just show up at my farm and whisk me away to goodness knows where. This had better be good..."

"Oh, it's good, Mrs Muckleton," Finbar chuckled. "You needn't worry about that. Right ho - you can open 'em now!"

Mrs Muckleton had not been holding out any great hopes that the farmer's so-called 'surprise' would be anything to write home about. She had known him ever since they had been children at the village school together and he had never, in all this time, succeeded in impressing her once. Indeed, it was the fact that her expectations were so low that made the sight that greeted her when she opened her eyes all the more amazing...

"Goodness me!" she gushed. "It's a *beach!* How *splendid!* And you did all of this just to impress me?"

"Erm... Yes, Mrs Muckleton – of course I did," Finbar lied.

By now, the sun was beginning to set, casting a beautiful orange glow across the surface of the water.

"How *romantic!*" It had been Mrs Muckleton's intention to dine with Old Joe Baxter again that evening, but the discovery of this beach had instantly banished all thoughts of the other man from her mind. "Would it be ok if I go for a paddle?"

"*Of course*, my dear," Finbar leered. "As a matter of fact, I think I'll join you if that's ok."

And with these fateful words, he took her brawny hand in his and they wandered down to the water's edge...

Epilogue

Dusk was drawing in over Finbar's field. All was quiet; many of the animals and birds had already turned in for the night, whilst the nocturnal creatures had yet to awaken. Underneath the old sycamore tree, the figure of a horse could be seen silhouetted against the setting western sun.

"Norbert?" Colin called down from his lofty perch.

"Yes, Colin?" Norbert sounded worried; his feathery friend *never* sought out his company unless it was to give him a good telling-off. But when Colin's beaky face appeared among the leaves, he was surprised to see that it bore an expression which was *almost* friendly.

"Norbert," the bird chirruped. "I wish to thank you."

"Oh?"

"Yes Norbert. Today has been one of the best days of my life."

"Oh?"

"You know how I often tell you how much I disapprove of Delilah?"

"Yes Colin."

"How I view her as vain, self-obsessed and shallow?"

"Yes Colin."

"Then you will no doubt appreciate the sheer joy you gave me when you cleverly lured her into that bog."

"But I didn't mean..."

"But you did not rest there, Norbert. So eager were you to patch up our friendship, that you decided to treat me to a triple-whammy by luring two of my other enemies, Farmer Finbar and Mrs Muckleton, to the same sticky fate!"

"But..."

"The sight of them emerging from that bog like a pair of *Creatures from the Black Lagoon* is one that I shall cherish for a long, long time…"

"Yes but…"

"Norbert - I have known you ever since you were a tiny foal, and until now, it has always been my firm belief that I would never have occasion to utter these words."

"But..."

"Norbert – You are a *GENIUS!*"

The End

Other titles in the
"Norbert the Horse" series

Norbert

Christmas with Norbert

Norbert to the Rescue!

Norbert's Spooky Night

Norbert - The Collection

www.norbertthehorse.com

Other titles by James Sutherland

Ticklesome Tales

Princess Petrina and the Witch's Curse
(featuring Norbert!)

Ernie

Frogarty the Witch

Roger the Frog

The Further Adventures of Roger the Frog

The Tale of the Miserous Mip

Jimmy Black and the Curse of Poseidon

Visit **www.jamessutherlandbooks.com**
for more information and all the latest news!

About the Author

James Sutherland was born in Stoke-on-Trent, England, many, many, many years ago. So long ago, in fact, that he can't remember a single thing about it. The son of a musician, he moved around lots as a youngster, attending schools in the Isle of Man and Spain before returning to Stoke where he lurked until the age of 18. After going on to gain a French degree at Bangor University, North Wales, he toiled at a variety of regular office jobs before making a daring escape through a fire exit in order to concentrate on writing silly nonsense full-time. Happily married, James lives with his wife and daughter in a small but perfectly formed market town in Staffordshire. In his spare time, James enjoys playing his guitar, reading history books, and discussing the deep, philosophical mysteries of life with his goldfish, Tiffany.

Printed in Great Britain
by Amazon